Cowboy Welles

Lauren Seiler and Pam Duke

XULON PRESS

Cowboy Welles
by Lauren Seiler and Pam Duke

Printed in the United States of America

ISBN 9781498447942

www.xulonpress.com

Illustrations by: D.W. Murray

D.W. Murray is a former Disney Animation artist, whose screen credits include Mulan, Tarzan, Lilo &Stitch, and Brother Bear. He is a graduate of the Rhode Island School of Design, a classically trained portrait artist who has painted the governor's portrait in Rhode Island which hangs in the R.I. State House. He is a former fashion illustrator whose work has been displayed in Vogue, Town & Country, The Boston Herald and Boston Globe.

Cowboy Welles is up and ready to ride.

He puts on his boots and runs outside.

He's looking for his horse, Pepper, around the farm…

Look! There he is in the big, red barn.

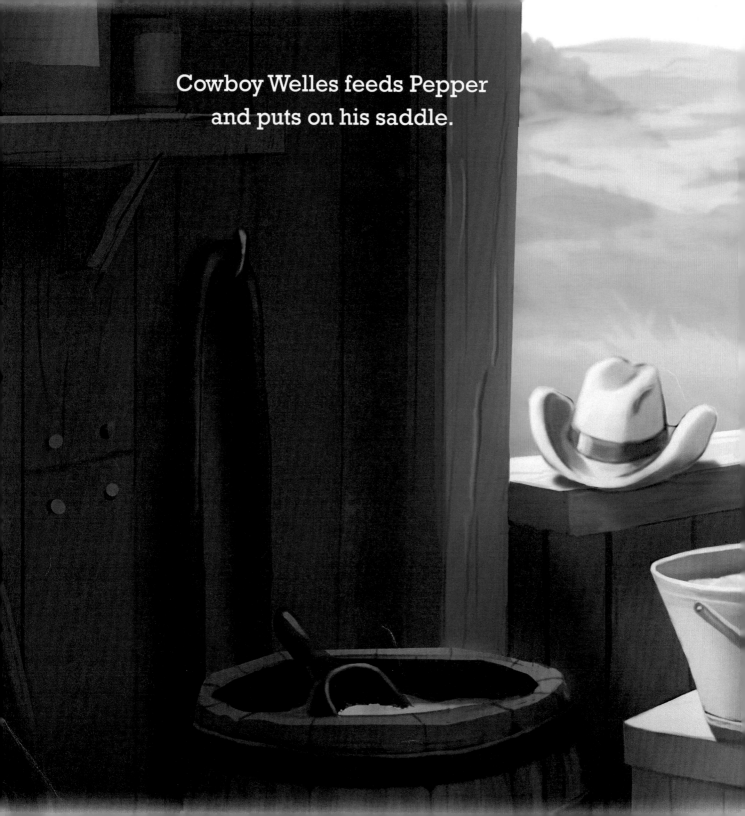

Cowboy Welles feeds Pepper
and puts on his saddle.

Their chore for the day
is herding the cattle.

9

They ride up the hill and spot a log.

A peek inside finds Marley the dog.

They now have their team
to work all day,

But working with friends feels more like play.

The hot, summer sun is high in the sky. Let's find the cows…. Do you want to try?

How many cows do you see?

"Woof woof woof." Marley picks up speed.

Cowboy Welles lets her take the lead.

They herd the cattle and move them along...

To the cow pens, where they belong.

Cowboy Welles leaps off Pepper and runs to shut the gate.

"We wouldn't want any of the cows to escape!"

YIPPEE!
It's a job well done for the cowboy team!

It's the end of the day, and
the work is complete.

They head back to the barn to enjoy a bath and a treat.

Splish! Splash!
The animals get a bath.

Taking care of your pets
is the cowboy and cowgirl way.

Treat them with respect, each and every day!

CPSIA information can be obtained
at www.ICGtesting.com
Printed in the USA
LVXC02n0038071215
465654LV00002B/2

* 9 7 8 1 4 9 8 4 4 7 9 4 2 *